Layla
the Cotton Candy
Fairy

Special thanks to Sue Mongredien

ISBN 978-0-545-60536-6

12 11 10 9 8 7 6 5 4 3 2 1   14 15 16 17 18 19/0

Printed in the U.S.A.   40

This edition first printing, March 2014

Layla
the Cotton Candy Fairy

by Daisy Meadows

SCHOLASTIC INC.

The Fairyland Palace

Candy Land

Goblins' ice cream truck

Market booths

Charlie's ice cream truck

Kirsty's House

Wetherbury Village

I have a plan to make a mess
And cause the fairies much distress.
I'm going to take their charms away
And make my dreams come true today!

I'll build a castle made of sweets,
And ruin the fairies' silly treats.
I just don't care how much they whine,
Their cakes and candies will be mine!

Contents

Wheeeee!

Kirsty Tate smiled as she began climbing
the steps up the giant slide with her best
friend, Rachel Walker. Today she felt
like the luckiest girl in the whole world!
Not only was it her birthday, but she was
at the Wetherbury Park Fair with
Rachel—and the sun was beaming

down, too. Best of all, she and Rachel were in the middle of another wonderful magical fairy adventure. This time, they were helping the Sugar and Spice Fairies!

"It's a long way up," Rachel commented from behind Kirsty as they climbed the steps. "We'll be able to see for miles from the top."

"Yes," Kirsty agreed. Then she lowered her voice. "We might even be able to see a fairy from up there!" She crossed her fingers hopefully at the thought. Meeting

another fairy would make her birthday absolutely perfect!

It was spring break and so far it had been a very exciting couple of days. At the beginning of the week, Honey the Candy Fairy had surprised them by appearing in a pile of candy in Kirsty's bedroom. She needed the girls' help to stop Jack Frost, who was up to his terrible tricks again. This time, he'd stolen the Sugar and Spice Fairies' magic charms! He was using them to help build himself an enormous Candy Castle.

The seven Sugar and Spice Fairies worked very hard to make sure that candy and treats in Fairyland and the human world tasted scrumptious. Without the fairies' magic charms, sweet things didn't taste good at all. Even

worse, today was the annual Treat Day
in Fairyland. The fairy king and queen
wouldn't be able to give their traditional
treat baskets to the other fairies unless all
seven charms were safely returned.

Kirsty and Rachel had been helping
the Sugar and Spice Fairies track down
their magic charms. So far, they'd found
five: the lollipop, ice cream, cupcake,
cocoa bean, and cookie charms. Now
there were just two fairies missing their
charms — Layla the Cotton Candy
Fairy and Nina the Birthday Cake
Fairy. And with Kirsty's birthday party
planned for that afternoon, she really
hoped they could help both fairies
before it was too late!

Just then, Kirsty reached the top of the

steps and let out a
gasp. "Wow!"
she said. "You
can see the whole
fair from up here!"

Wetherbury Park was usually a quiet,
calm place, full of dog-walkers and
joggers, but today it was full of bustle
and noise. It seemed like the whole
village had come to the fair today!

"There's the teacup ride," Rachel said,
pointing it out. "Oh, and the ball toss is
right next to it."

"I can see my mom and dad!" Kirsty
cried, waving excitedly. "Look, they're
over by the cotton candy stand. I hope
that means we can have some when we
meet up with them."

"Ooh, yes," Rachel agreed. "And there's the mirror maze, I love those," she added. "But I don't see any fairies. Or goblins . . ."

Kirsty's eyes narrowed as she scanned the crowds of people and the booths and attractions below, looking for a flash of green. The goblins were Jack Frost's helpers, and they were always causing trouble. But, like Rachel, she couldn't see a single one at the fair today.

"Ready when you are," said the man running the giant slide. "Are you girls riding together, or separately?"

"Together!" the girls cried, then grinned. *Everything* was more fun when they did it together!

They squeezed onto a long, scratchy mat. Rachel sat behind Kirsty with her arms around Kirsty's waist. Then they pushed off and went zooming away down the twisty slide.

"*Wheeee!*" cried Rachel happily, her hair streaming out behind her.

"I feel like I'm flying!" Kirsty laughed, the air rushing past her face.

Rachel blinked as she spotted a tiny glowing object in the air beside them.

She rubbed her eyes and peered closer,
then beamed. "Well, someone here really
is flying," she said, pointing out the
sparkling figure at their side. "Look,
Kirsty, it's Layla the Cotton Candy
Fairy!"

A Sticky Situation

Layla was a very pretty little fairy. She had blonde hair with pink-tipped ends, as if it had been dipped in strawberry sauce. She wore a bright pink, flowery dress with a pale pink leather jacket and matching pink polka-dot shoes. Even her cute ankle socks were pink!

"Hello there," she said, fluttering over to land on Kirsty's hand, "and a very happy birthday to you, Kirsty!"

"Thank you!" replied Kirsty breathlessly, as they hurtled around another corner. "I'm sure it's going to be an even better birthday now that you're

here. Have you found your magic cotton candy charm yet?" "No," Layla said, darting into Kirsty's pocket, "but I'm sure it's somewhere at the fair. Would you two mind helping me look for it?"

Neither Rachel nor Kirsty could reply for a moment as they zipped off the end of the slide. They staggered to

their feet, giggling and feeling a little
dizzy.

"That was so much fun!" Rachel said.
"And of course we'll help you, Layla."

"Thank you," Layla said,
her eyes twinkling
as she peeked out
of Kirsty's pocket.
"That *was*
fun, wasn't
it? Almost
as good as
flying."
Then her
little nose
twitched.
"Ooh, I smell
cotton candy," she said happily.

"The best smell in the world!"

"There's my mom and dad," Kirsty said, waving as she spotted them nearby. "And look what they're holding!"

"Cotton candy," Rachel said with a laugh. "Perfect!"

"Hello there," Mrs. Tate said as Kirsty and Rachel ran up. "That looked exciting."

"We thought you might like to share this," said Mr. Tate, passing Kirsty a huge stick of cotton candy. It was pale pink and glittering with sugar.

"Thank you," Kirsty said, trying not to giggle as she thought about Layla hiding in her jacket pocket. "I was just thinking I'd like some yummy cotton candy! You must have read my mind!"

"We're going to get a cup of coffee now," Mrs. Tate went on. "Should we meet you back here in half an hour?"

"Sounds perfect," Rachel replied. "See you later. And thanks for the cotton candy!"

"Yum," Kirsty said, as her parents walked away with a wave. "This looks delicious."

Layla popped her head out and eyed the cotton candy. "It looks great, but remember, it might not taste that way," she said. "Without my magic cotton candy charm, I'm not

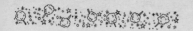

sure how good it'll be. Maybe I should test it first?"

"Okay," Kirsty agreed. "I'll break a piece off for you." She pinched the top of the cotton candy, expecting a bit to pull away easily in her fingers. But instead, it felt as hard as a rock. "That's strange," she said, pulling again. "It's really hard."

Layla bit her lip. "That doesn't sound good," she said. Rachel also tried to snap off a clump of cotton candy, but she couldn't manage to do it, either. "We'll break our teeth if we bite

into this," she said with a frown. "And so
will anyone else who buys it!"

"Oh, dear," Layla said. She pointed her
wand at the cotton
candy and
murmured a
few magic
words. The
cotton candy
sparkled all
over with pink
and silver light.
Then a fairy-size
piece of it broke
away, flew through the
air, and landed in Layla's hand. She
nibbled at it carefully and then wrinkled
her face in disgust. "*Yuck!* It tastes
horrible," she cried. "Jack Frost ruined it!"

17

Rachel and Kirsty felt sorry for Layla.
She looked so upset! Then Rachel spotted
three boys on the teacup ride nearby.
They were all digging into enormous
sticks of rainbow-striped cotton candy,
and they seemed to be eating it just fine.
"Look! Not all of the cotton candy is
ruined," she said, pointing out the boys
to Kirsty and Layla. "Maybe the stick
your parents bought was just a bad one."

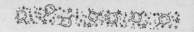

Layla peered thoughtfully at the
rainbow cotton candy. "It does look
good," she agreed. "Soft, fluffy, sticky,
and delicious. Just the way cotton candy
should be. And they're certainly
enjoying it!"

The boys' faces were hidden by the
huge sticks of cotton candy, but just then
their teacup spun around. The girls were
able to see them more clearly. Rachel,
Kirsty, and Layla all gasped as they
noticed how green the boys' skin was,
and what pointy noses they had, too.

"Goblins!" they cried.

19

Chasing Rainbows

Once the three friends had spotted the
first group of goblins, they suddenly
began seeing them all over the place!
There were goblins at the ring toss,
tripping over their own big green feet as
they clumsily threw the rings. There
were goblins trying and failing to win a
big teddy bear at the hook-a-duck game.
And there were goblins lining up for the

haunted house, looking nervous at the screams and yells coming from inside. But the best part was that every single one of the goblins was carrying a huge stick of fluffy, rainbow-striped cotton candy.

"Where are they getting them all from?" Kirsty wondered aloud.

"Someone is obviously making yummy cotton candy *somewhere*," Rachel replied, glancing around.

"And I bet whoever it is has my magic charm," Layla added. "If we can just get it back, then I could make *all* the cotton candy taste good again." She fluttered out of Kirsty's pocket. "Maybe we'll be able to look around the fair more quickly if you two are both fairies. What do you think?"

"*Ooh,* yes! Definitely," Kirsty said right away. She felt giddy with excitement as she and Rachel ducked behind a popcorn stand so that nobody would see them. She loved being a fairy. What a fun birthday treat!

Layla waved her wand, and a stream of glittery pink fairy dust swirled out. *It looks just like tiny clouds of cotton candy,* Rachel thought with a smile as the sparkly dust shimmered around her and Kirsty. In the next moment, the girls felt themselves shrinking smaller and smaller until they were fairy-size, too, with glimmering wings on their backs.

With just a few flutters, they were
sailing up into the air. Both girls had
huge grins on their face. Being able to
fly was way better than any giant slide!

"Now," said Layla,
peering down
eagerly at the fair
below. "Keep
your eyes peeled
for signs of
anyone making or
selling the rainbow-
striped cotton candy."

The three fairies began searching all
around the fair. There was so much to
see and so many people that they had to
look very carefully! "Well, there's the
pink cotton candy stand," Kirsty said,
pointing down at it. "That must be

where my mom and dad bought the horrible cotton candy for us."

The stall was deserted. "At least nobody's buying anything from there now," Layla said with a little shudder. "I would hate for anyone else to find out how awful it tastes."

But she'd spoken too soon. Just then, a customer walked up to the stand.

"Oh, no!" said Rachel. "Do you think we should warn him somehow?"

"We can't let anyone see us," Layla reminded her. "But let's fly closer and see what happens. I might be able to use some fairy dust to make his cotton candy taste a little better."

The three friends fluttered down and landed on the top of the cotton candy stand. They could see that the customer

was wearing a bright green clown suit complete with a curly wig, enormous shoes, and a bright green round nose.

Moments later, the clown walked away with two big pink sticks of cotton candy.

"Oh, no," Kirsty said. "He's in for a horrible surprise now. Poor clown!"

Layla raised her wand. "Maybe I can quickly work some magic on that cotton candy," she murmured. "Now, let me see . . ."

But before Layla could come up with a spell, something very strange happened. The cotton candy began to transform all by itself! It went from the hard, pink cotton candy that the clown had bought into fluffy, rainbow-striped cotton candy!

"Wow," Rachel said, impressed. "Your magic worked so fast, Layla. That was great!"

Layla looked startled. "I didn't do anything," she said. "Either that clown has magic powers, or—"

She stopped talking and looked at the clown in surprise. He'd just taken an enormous bite of the soft, sweet cotton candy. And as he did, his clown nose had popped off and fallen to the ground! The fairies couldn't help

noticing how green and pointy his real nose was.

"He's a goblin!" Kirsty gasped.

"Yes, and if he's able to make the bad

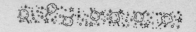

cotton candy taste good, he must have my magic charm," Layla realized. Her eyes grew wide with excitement. "So *that's* where all the cotton candy is coming from!"

Mirror, Mirror

Just then, the three fairy friends heard excited voices.

"Look, it's a clown!"

"And he has some of the rainbow cotton candy!"

Rachel, Kirsty, and Layla peered down to see a group of kids approaching. They all stared at the clown with wide eyes. A boy in a red T-shirt stepped forward.

"Excuse me," he said politely, "we were just wondering . . ."

The clown looked annoyed to be disturbed. "Go away," he snapped. "Can't you see I'm busy?"

"But we've been looking everywhere for the rainbow cotton candy," a girl with braids piped up. "We just wanted to know where you bought yours."

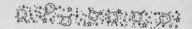

"I'm not telling," the clown snapped. "And I'm not sharing, either, so don't ask. Now, get lost!"

The kids looked disappointed. "But we only wanted to know—" the boy tried again, but the clown had turned on his heel and stomped away.

"Wait!" called a girl in a purple shirt. "Come back, please!"

The kids followed the clown, who made an impatient growling sound when he realized they were behind him.

"Go away!" he said. "Leave me alone!"

He dashed into the nearby

mirror maze, clearly hoping to lose them.

"Come on," Layla said as he vanished.
"We can't let him get away. Let's follow
him."

The fairies
fluttered
into the
mirror
maze,
making sure
they flew up near the ceiling so they
wouldn't be spotted. The three kids ran
after the clown, but quickly lost their
way in the confusing maze.

"Where *is* he?" the fairies heard the
boy cry.

"We just wanted to buy some cotton
candy!" one of the girls said. "Why did
he run away like that?"

The fairies zipped through the maze until they caught up with the clown. He was muttering angrily to himself. "Annoying children!" he complained. "They're as bad as the other goblins, pestering me all the time for more cotton candy. The goblins know I'm supposed to be taking it back for Jack Frost's Candy Castle."

Layla, Kirsty, and Rachel froze in midair at the mention of Jack Frost. They all listened carefully as the goblin kept grumbling to himself.

"He wants to use it for cotton candy

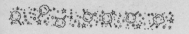

hedges in the shape of his head, he says.
But as fast as I get the cotton candy, it
gets eaten. There'll just be tiny cotton
candy bushes at this rate," he muttered.
"And here I am, working nonstop! This
magic charm is more trouble than it's
worth. Just my luck!"

"Jack Frost wants to use my delicious
cotton candy to make
hedges," Layla hissed,
looking indignant.
"Honestly!"

"Well, now we
know the goblin
definitely has the
charm, at least," Rachel
whispered. "So all we have to do is get it
back."

"Maybe we could—" Kirsty began,

but she broke off as they heard the kids approaching again.

"He must have gone *this* way," the boy was saying.

"Come on, we have to find him," a girl added. "He can't be far away."

Hearing the kid's voices, a look of panic appeared on the clown goblin's face. "Oh, great," he grumbled, rushing forward. Unfortunately, he ran straight into a mirror! He had reached a dead end. "Oh, *no!*" he moaned, as the kids' voices grew louder. Any moment now, the kids would

track him down, and he would be
trapped!

Rachel had an idea. She bravely flew
down, right in front of the clown's face.
"Hi," she said cheerfully. "I have a
suggestion to make."

The clown jumped
when he saw
Rachel and all
her fairy
reflections in
the mirrors. "Go
away!" he hissed,
swatting at her with his
sticks of cotton candy.
"Children . . . fairies . . . Why can't you
all just buzz off?"

"I can help you," Rachel insisted,

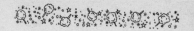

darting out of reach. "We can all help you."

Kirsty and Layla flew down then, too, dancing lightly through the air in front of him.

The clown looked fed up. "Why did I ever come into this silly maze?" he complained as he searched for an escape. "I have no idea why *you* came in here, but I can tell you why *we* did," Layla retorted, quick as a flash. "To get my cotton candy charm back!"

"Never," the clown snarled. "It's mine now! Jack Frost said so."

"Ah, but what if we could help you get away from the kids?" Rachel said. "Would you give it to us then?"

"We could make a deal," Kirsty added quickly. "You said yourself that having the charm is too much hard work, after all."

"And I'm sure you don't want to be trapped here by all those noisy kids . . ." Layla coaxed, as their voices grew louder.

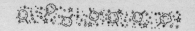

Then the boy in the red T-shirt appeared a few feet away. The boy whooped with triumph and pointed at the clown. "There he is!" he cried. "I found him!"

Boing!

The clown gulped as he saw all the kids charging toward him.

"Oh, all right, all right!" he muttered to the fairies. "You can have the charm. Just don't let them catch me and take all my cotton candy!"

Layla waved her wand and burst into action. A new mirror appeared in a bright flurry of pink sparkles. It sliced through the short hallway between the kids and the clown.

"Whoa, that was weird," the fairies heard the boy say to his friends. "I'm *sure* he was there a minute ago. It's like he just magically disappeared!"

The clown chuckled with relief. "Nice work, fairy," he said.

But Layla wasn't finished! Two seconds later, one of the mirrors behind the clown vanished, giving him an easy escape route through the maze. "There," she said. "How's that?"

"Wow," the clown marveled,

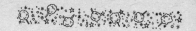

his eyes boggling at her amazing magic. "Thanks for that." And he turned and dashed away, his huge clown shoes slapping against the floor.

"Wait a minute," Layla called, flying after him. "Don't forget our deal. You have to give me my charm back now."

"Not a chance," he yelled over his shoulder. "So long!"

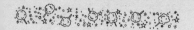

"Hey!" Rachel cried. "That's not fair.
You agreed!"

The clown just laughed and kept
running. He ran all the way out of the
maze and through the fair, still clutching
the cotton candy. Kirsty, Rachel, and
Layla flew as fast as they could after
him, but they couldn't quite catch up.

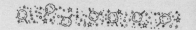

"We can't let him get away," Layla said breathlessy. "Keep flying, girls!"

The clown ran out of the fair and into a small group of trees at the edge of the park. The fairies followed him into a clearing. There they saw a huge mound of rainbow-colored cotton candy!

"Wow," Rachel said, staring in surprise. "It's like a cotton candy mountain."

The clown turned around, hearing her. "Yes, and you're not getting any of it," he told the fairies sharply. "I worked my socks off collecting this for Jack Frost's hedges. It's the best cotton candy in town." He made a face at Layla. "I think you should let me keep your cotton candy charm, actually," he went on. "I'm much better at making this stuff than any fairy."

"Oh, really?" said Layla, annoyed.

"Yeah, really," he retorted, climbing up the colorful mountain to dump his

new cotton candy on
the very top. "Look
at this," he said,
bouncing on his toes
and springing
back up. "Super-
soft and super-
bouncy. It's
perfect!"

Layla was
about to
argue with
him, but just then, Kirsty had an idea.
She quickly spoke up. "That *does* look
bouncy," she said admiringly. "I bet it
makes a great trampoline. Can I have
a try?"

"Oh, yes! Me, too!" Rachel cried.
"Please?"

The clown sneered down at them. "No way," he told them. "This is *my* cotton candy mountain. If anyone's going to bounce on it, it's me. Watch this!"

He gave an enormous leap and boinged straight back up again. "Ha-ha!" he laughed. "This is *fuuuun!*"

Layla sighed. "I can't bear to watch," she said. "He's ruining the only good cotton candy at the whole fair with those huge, dirty feet of his."

"Wait," Kirsty urged in a low voice. "I'm hoping all the bouncing might

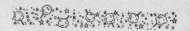

shake the cotton candy charm loose if it's in his pocket. You never know."

"Good idea!" Layla smiled. "Let's hope so."

Unfortunately, the magic charm didn't fly out of the clown's pocket— because just then, he tripped on his big clown shoes. "Whoa!" he yelled as he toppled over and went rolling down the mountain. "Help!"

Rachel, Kirsty, and Layla couldn't help giggling as he rolled down. Strands of

sticky cotton candy wound around him
as he went. By the time he reached the
bottom, he was in the middle of a tight
cotton candy ball, with his head sticking
out of one end and his clown feet out the
other!

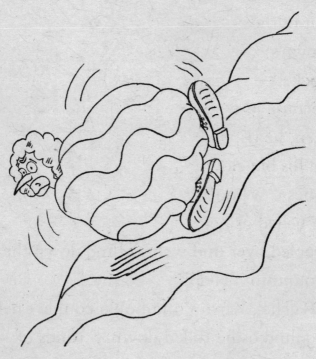

Layla grinned and raised an eyebrow. "Whoops," she said to the clown as he kicked and hollered. "How in the world are you going to get out of *that*?"

Cotton Candy Capture!

"Help!" the clown called, thrashing his head around as he struggled to free himself. It was no use! He was completely stuck in the ball of cotton candy. He just rolled a little from side to side, like a beetle on its back.

"Help?"
echoed Rachel,
pretending to
think. "But last
time we helped
you, you didn't
keep your end
of the deal. Why
would we help you
again?"

"It's true," Layla said. "If you'd given
me the cotton candy charm the first
time, like you promised, we might be
willing to help you out now, but . . ."

She left the sentence hanging, and the
clown let out a groan.

"Oh, all right," he grumbled. "If I give
you the charm now, will you help me
out of this cotton candy ball?"

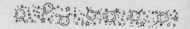

Kirsty grinned. "We will," she said. "But this time, you give us the charm *first*."

The clown heaved a big sigh. "It's in my shoe," he muttered. "Help yourself."

Layla quickly turned Kirsty and Rachel back into girls, and they ran around the cotton candy ball to the goblin's feet. 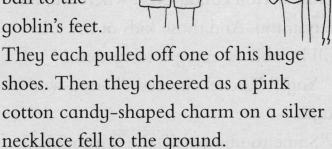 They each pulled off one of his huge shoes. Then they cheered as a pink cotton candy-shaped charm on a silver necklace fell to the ground.

"Hooray!" cried Layla, swooping

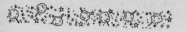

down toward it. As
soon as she touched
the charm, it
shrank to fairy-
size. She
fastened it
around her
neck. There
was a sudden
flash of bright pink light, and the little
fairy grinned. "My cotton candy magic
is working again," she said happily.
"Now cotton candy everywhere should
be yummy. And those kids at the fair
will be able to enjoy a tasty treat!"

"Yay!" Rachel cheered. "Good work,
Layla."

"Same to you two!" the fairy replied.

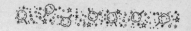

"I couldn't have done it without your help, that's for sure."

A grumpy cough came from the clown. "Ahem," he said. "Aren't you forgetting something? Our deal?"

Layla's eyes sparkled mischievously. "A fairy never breaks a promise," she said. "Unlike *some* people . . ." She waved her wand, and magic sparkles puffed out of the tip.

As soon as the fairy magic touched the huge ball of cotton candy, it began to

dissolve, twirling up into the air like smoke. After a moment, the clown was free! There was just one small clump of cotton candy left, in the shape of Jack Frost's head.

The clown looked unhappy when he saw it, but muttered a thank-you and trudged away. "I hope Jack Frost won't be *too* angry with me," the girls heard him saying as he went, clutching the cotton candy.

"Thanks again," Layla said, spinning happily in midair. "I'd better get back to Fairyland now. I need to make some special cotton candy for the Treat Day baskets. If I hurry, I'll just be in time! But before I go, these are for you." She waved her wand, and two big sticks

of fluffy rainbow cotton candy appeared
in Kirsty's and Rachel's hands.
"Good-bye!"

"Good-bye!" called Kirsty and
Rachel. "And thank you!" They waved
as Layla zipped away. Soon she was just
a tiny speck of glowing light against the
blue sky.

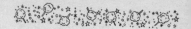

"We'd better go meet my mom and dad now," Kirsty said, noticing the time. She took a bite of her cotton candy as they walked. "*Oooh!* It's so fluffy and gooey."

"Yum," said Rachel, enjoying a mouthful of hers, too. "It's the best cotton candy I've ever had. And look how  sparkly it is—definitely a fairy magic special!"

"Helping Layla was really fun," Kirsty said happily as they made their way back through the fairground. "And now there's

only one Sugar and Spice Fairy left to help."

Rachel grinned. "Nina the Birthday Cake Fairy," she remembered. "We have to help her get her magic charm back, Kirsty, so that all birthday cakes taste yummy—including yours!"

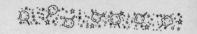

"You're right," said Kirsty. She linked arms with Rachel and giggled. "But no matter what happens, so far this has definitely been my most exciting birthday ever!"

Rachel and Kirsty found Lisa, Esme, Coco, Clara, Madeline, and Layla's missing magic charms. Now it's time for them to help

Nina
the Birthday Cake Fairy!

Join their next adventure in this special sneak peek. . . .

Cake Calamity

"What an amazing birthday this has been!" said Kirsty Tate, twirling happily in the middle of the sidewalk.

"It's been the most fun birthday ever," agreed her best friend, Rachel Walker. "I've enjoyed it just as much as you, even though it's not even MY birthday!"

Rachel was visiting the Tate family for spring break. Right now, they were walking home from Wetherbury Park with Kirsty's parents. They had been celebrating Kirsty's birthday at the village fair!

"So, what's been the best thing about your birthday so far?" asked Mr. Tate.

Kirsty threw her hands into the air. "I can't decide!" she said with a laugh. "Everything has been perfect. Rachel's here, Aunt Helen gave us a tour of Candy Land, and we had a great time at the fair."

"Well, your birthday is about to get even better," said Mrs. Tate, raising an eyebrow.

Kirsty stopped and looked at her parents and Rachel. Their eyes were all sparkling with happiness.

"We have another birthday surprise for you," Mr. Tate added.

Kirsty looked at their smiling faces in excitement. What could it be?

"You have to tell me what the surprise is!" she pleaded.

Rachel shook her head. "That would ruin it," she said. "Come on, let's hurry back to your house."

The girls held hands and rushed ahead.

"It's really hard to keep secrets from you," Rachel said breathlessly. "We usually share all our secrets!"

In fact, the girls shared one of the biggest secrets imaginable. They were friends with the fairies! Their latest magical adventures were some of the most thrilling they'd ever had.

"My birthday would be absolutely

perfect if we could just help the last Sugar
and Spice Fairy get her charm back from
Jack Frost," said Kirsty.

Two days ago, Jack Frost and his
goblins had stolen the magic charms that
belonged to the seven Sugar and Spice
Fairies. Honey the Candy Fairy had
come to ask the girls for their help.

"We've already found six of the magic
charms," said Rachel proudly. "There's
just one more to find."

The Sugar and Spice Fairies needed
their charms to create all kinds of
delicious sweet treats in Fairyland and
the human world. But Jack Frost wanted
all the treats for his own special
project—a giant Candy Castle! He gave
the Sugar and Spice Fairies' charms to
his goblins for safekeeping, and ordered

them to bring back all the yummy treats from the human world.

"The worst part is that today is Treat Day in Fairyland," said Kirsty. "If Queen Titania and King Oberon don't have goodies to put in the fairies' treat baskets, Treat Day will have to be canceled!"

RAINBOW magic™

Which Magical Fairies Have You Met?

- ❑ The Rainbow Fairies
- ❑ The Weather Fairies
- ❑ The Jewel Fairies
- ❑ The Pet Fairies
- ❑ The Dance Fairies
- ❑ The Music Fairies
- ❑ The Sports Fairies
- ❑ The Party Fairies
- ❑ The Ocean Fairies
- ❑ The Night Fairies
- ❑ The Magical Animal Fairies
- ❑ The Princess Fairies
- ❑ The Superstar Fairies
- ❑ The Fashion Fairies
- ❑ The Sugar & Spice Fairies

SCHOLASTIC

Find all of your favorite fairy friends at
scholastic.com/rainbowmagic

HIT entertainment

RMFAIRY9